D0938185

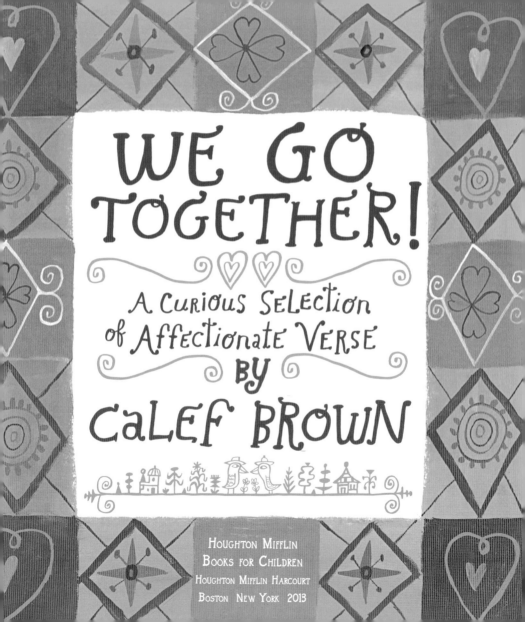

WE GO TOGETHER!

A Curious Selection of Affectionate Verse

BY

CALEF BROWN

HOUGHTON MIFFLIN
BOOKS FOR CHILDREN
HOUGHTON MIFFLIN HARCOURT
BOSTON NEW YORK 2013

For Anissa, Darwin, and Matilda

Houghton Mifflin Books for Children is an imprint of Houghton
Mifflin Harcourt Publishing Company.

www.hmhbooks.com

The text of this book is set in AgedBook.
The illustrations are done in acrylic.

Library of Congress Cataloging-in-Publication Data
is on file.
ISBN 978-0-547-72128-6
Manufactured in China
Leo 10 9 8 7 6 5 4 3 2 1
4500376175

Contents

Let's Go!

Come for a ride
on the handlebars
of a bicycle built for one.
I got the idea
from a movie I saw.
It looked like lots of fun.

We Go Together

We go together
like fingers and thumbs.
Basses and drums.
Pastries and crumbs.
We go together
like apples and plums.
Molars and gums.
Genuine chums.
Loyal amigos
with infinite sums
of friendship, affection,
and pure camaraderie.
We won the buddy lottery.

You Are Two (Kiwis)

I am, quite frequently,
reminded by thee
of a kiwi.
Either kind.
You have thin skin,
or rather, rind,
but mostly I find
that you're frightfully sweet.
You won't ever fly
but are light on your feet.
Your voice is enchanting.
The tone is so soft.
To some you're aloof
but to me you're aloft.

Totally!

We should *totally*
start a band together!
Let's call it Thunderbug!
Or Sandalfeather!
Maybe Bungee Lump?
No! Panda Weather!
We should *totally*
start a band together!

My Doorbell

You to me
are like an adorable doorbell.
You ring me up
and I race down the stairwell.
I skitter across sidewalks
and scamper under overpasses,
around the crowded street corners,
and through the hurried masses
with more
and more
and more pep.
Then I'm on your doorstep!

FBF

Forever,
we will be best friends,
even during the worst trends.
Remember that greenish phase?
Those were colorful days!
Our clothes were drab olives
and loud chartreuses.
We nibbled on limes
and concocted strange juices
with lettuce and kale.
We trained an iguana
to get us the mail.
My eardrums still hurt
from the noise that we made
performing at weddings
as "Emerald 'n' Jade."

Mirth Makers

Oh, the mirth we make!
Every day of life
is like a birthday cake.
We light it up
and blow it out.
We laugh and sing
and jump and shout.
No nap.
No coffee break.
Oh, the mirth we make!

Two Scallywags

You and I are scallywags.
Let us plan a caper!
We can build a UFO
and fool the local paper.
The two of us are quite the scamps,
although we're only six.
Hatching plots and pulling pranks–
we play a lot of tricks.
You and I are scallywags.
Let us have adventures!
We can climb an apple tree
and hide the teacher's dentures.

Scrootin' Eyes

Sometimes I catch you
giving me the "scrootin' eyes."
Your eyes go wide
like two pies,
then slowly narrow.
You're a cat.
I'm a sparrow.
But then you crack a smile
and your nose wiggles,
quickly followed
by one of *those* giggles.
The ones that show your dimple-wrinkles.
Then my heart twinkles.

Thank You

My mind was in a panic,
but you remained calm,
ready to do battle
with the splinter in my palm.
Utilizing tweezers
and a tube of minty balm,
you quickly removed it.
My hand felt prickly
until you soothed it.

Roller Buddy

Before we met,
I was *such*
a timid roller skater.
Only on rugs,
or in an elevator.
But you, like a pal,
gave me pep talks
and newer skates.
Now I do figure eights
and navigate the sewer grates.
Gone are the scrapes
and wobbled bones.
No more fear of cobblestones!

Taking Note

You always remember
the type of tea I enjoy,
how much milk,
which spoon to employ,
the correct teapot,
and whether to steep it or not.

Noticing things,
about me, especially,
seems to be your specialty.

Laughers

I cackle
and you chortle.
Together we *chorkle.*
It sounds like two porpoises
sharing a snorkel.

You guffaw
and I giggle.
Together we *guffle.*
It sounds like two badger cubs
having a scuffle.

My Closer

It never bothered me—
I find it sweet—
the way you complete
not only my sentences
but my paragraphs too.
"I love," I will say,
"... *the giraffes at the zoo,*"
you respond.
"*I'm also fond
of the anaconda,
the koi pond,
and the pandas as well.*"
I think that it's swell
when you pick up my thread.
Always a pleasure
to hear what I said.

Without a doubt, my favorite color is BLUE! Royal Blue, Robin's Egg Blue, Ultra-marine. What's not to like? It's the color of beautiful skies and malamute eyes.
I also love Red. I do.

Snow Globes

Whenever you travel
and off you fly
to Europe, say,
or Uruguay,
you always bring
a snow globe home.
A gift for me.
A plastic dome
from Nome, Alaska,
Lincoln, Nebraska,
or Toronto, Ontario.
Each with a snowy scenario—
a tiny diorama.
The one from Peru
has Machu Picchu
and a llama.

Backup

If someone makes a crack
or puts me down,
you back me up
and stick around.
Always there
when I get in a tangle.
I lean on you
at a steep angle–
I'm so inclined.
A better friend
I'll never find.

Because of You

I was once
a half-emptyer.
Now I'm a half-fuller.
Because of you—
the together-puller.
So if I should smile
and say something sunny,
don't look at me funny
or act surprised.
Because of you,
I'm optimized.

Your Smile

Your smile
is sufficiently bright
to turn a winter night
to a summer day.
It could make a grand slam
from a double play,
or a peaceful dove
from a bird of prey.

Your smile
quite easily
could warm the Arctic sea,
which wouldn't be good–
no siree.
It's just a silly allegory–
a tall tale or a small story–
to illuminate
for a short while
the greatness of,
the sweetness of,
your smile.